For *my father* C. Mc.

First published in the United States, 1982,
by Philomel Books,
a division of The Putnam Publishing Group,
200 Madison Avenue,
New York, N.Y. 10016.

Published in Great Britain by Walker Books, Ltd.
Printed in Italy.

Library of Congress Cataloging in Publication Data
Hoban, Russell.
   The flight of Bembel Rudzuk.
   Summary: The squidgerino squelcher, created by Bembel
Rudzuk, the wizard, annoys the princess.
[1. Fairy tales. 2. Monsters—Fiction]
I. McNaughton, Colin, ill. II. Title
PZ8.H63FL 1982   [Fic]   81-21056
ISBN 399-20888-7   AACR 2
ISBN 0-399-61198-3 (lib. bdg.)

The Flight of Bembel Rudzuk

RUSSELL HOBAN

PICTURES BY COLIN McNAUGHTON

PHILOMEL BOOKS

Text (c) 1982 by Russell Hoban
Illustrations (c) 1982 by Colin McNaughton

The squidgerino squelcher was put together
by the wizard Bembel Rudzuk.
Bembel Rudzuk made up three jars of monster
powder, then he added twelve buckets of
water and Splosh! there was the squidgerino
squelcher. It slobbered and it moaned, it
left a loathsome track behind it.
Everyone was terrified, everyone ran off
and left the princess all unguarded.

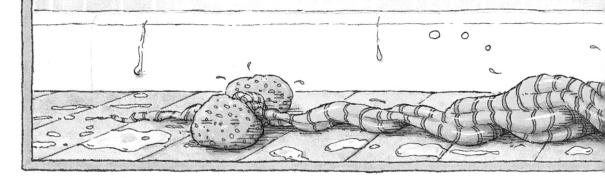

The squidgerino squelcher chased her up a
tower, then it crept around the bottom of the
tower slobbering and moaning.

The princess looked at the mess the squidgerino squelcher was making and she became rather cross. "Where'd this monster come from?" she said. "And who's going to clean up after it?"

The front half of the squidgerino squelcher
said, "It was Bembel Rudzuk's . . ."
"Idea," said the back half.
"Where is Bembel Rudzuk?" said the princess.
"He's gone," said the front half. "He left
a little while ago on a flying . . ."

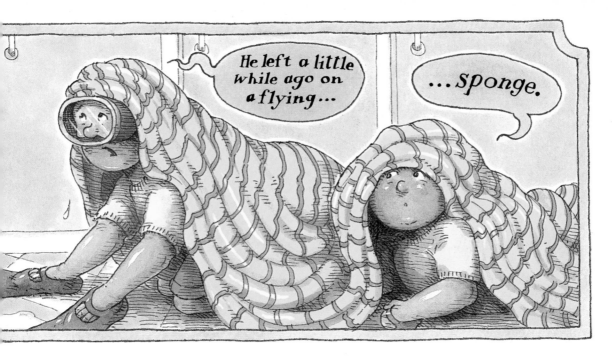

"Sponge," said the back half.
"Where is he now?" said the princess.
The front half said, "He's out somewhere making . . ."
"Rain," said the back half.
"I'll make *him* rain," said the princess.
"Just wait till I catch up with him."

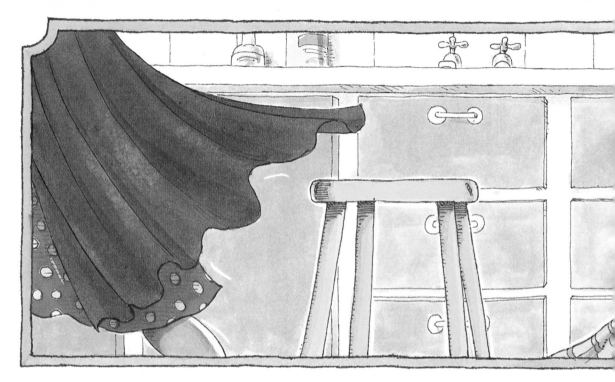

She put on her cloak of darkness and got ready to take off. "You get that floor cleaned up before I get back," she said to the squidgerino squelcher and Whoosh! she was gone.

"I don't see why we should clean up the whole

mess ourselves," said the front half to the back half.
"Let's find Bembel Rudzuk."
Off they slopped and slithered, slobbering and
moaning, squelching and groaning through the
desert and the mountains seeking Bembel Rudzuk.

Bembel Rudzuk was cruising at ten thousand feet when he saw the princess close behind him. He parachuted down and landed in the deep and shadowy forest of Backgar Den.

"I must try to get to Gar Denshed before the
princess sees me," said Bembel Rudzuk.
"There are lots of good hiding places there."

The squidgerino squelcher was hot on
Bembel Rudzuk's trail.
"Where would you go if you were Bembel
Rudzuk?" said the front half to the back half.

"Gar Denshed," said the back half.
They got there quickly, opened the door,
and slipped inside.

"Bembel Rudzuk?" said the back half.
"Don't see him," said the front half, "but I
see a cheesecake."
"Smells good," said the back half.

The front half said, "If we were to cut off
just a little bit all down one side, do you
think she'd notice?"
"No," said the back half.

"What can we cut it with?" said the front half.
"Here's a saw," said a voice. It was Bembel Rudzuk.
He'd been hiding in a cluttered corner.

Quickly he sawed off a long narrow piece of
cheesecake, the front of the squidgerino
squelcher divided it into three equal parts, and
the back half had first choice.

"You know," said the front half, "that cheesecake *doesn't* look the same now."
"Saw off more," said the back half.
"He's right," said Bembel Rudzuk, and sawed off another piece of cheesecake.

When they had all eaten their second pieces,
the front half of the squidgerino squelcher said,
"That cheesecake looks even more different now,
it looks all small and funny-shaped."

"You're right," said Bembel Rudzuk. "I think maybe we should go back and clean up that mess we made as fast as we can. I don't want the princess to be mad at me for two things at once." Bembel Rudzuk and the squidgerino squelcher hurried back and cleaned up the mess.

Just as they finished, the princess arrived.
"It's nice to see the castle looking clean and
tidy again," said the princess. "Would you like
some cocoa?"
"Oh, yes, please," said everybody. "That would
be great."

"Would you like some cheesecake with your cocoa?"
said the princess.

"Ah!" said the two halves of the squidgerino squelcher.
"Um," said Bembel Rudzuk.

"Isn't this odd!" said the princess when she brought in the cheesecake. "It's quite a bit smaller and it's all raggedy along two sides. Do you suppose mice have been at it?"

"Squeak, squeak!" said the two halves of the
squidgerino squelcher.
"Squeak!" said Bembel Rudzuk.